big&SMALL

Original Korean text by Seok-ki Nam
Illustrations by Sang-wu Shin
Korean edition © Yeowon Media Co., Ltd.

This English edition published by Big & Small in 2015
by arrangement with Yeowon Media Co., Ltd.
English text edited by Joy Cowley
English edition © Big & Small 2015

ISBN: 978-1-921790-96-6

Printed in Korea

The Bremen Town Musicians

A story by the Brothers Grimm
retold by Joy Cowley
Illustrated by Sang-wu Shin

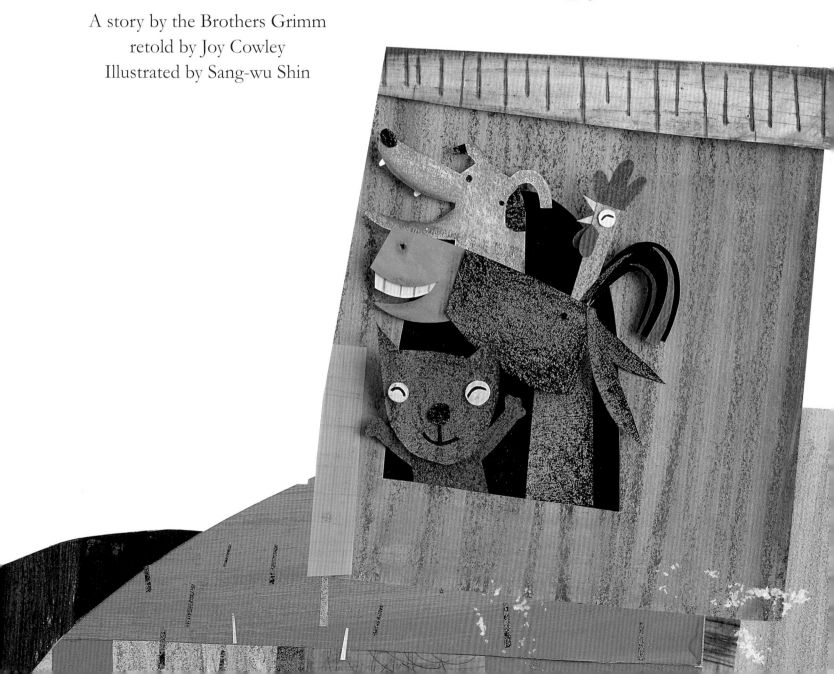

A long time ago, there was a donkey
who worked hard for his master.
But when the donkey grew old,
its master screamed at him, saying,
"I will get rid of this useless donkey."

The donkey sneaked away.
"I've worked hard all my life
and now my master doesn't want me,"
it said. "I will go to Bremen town
and become a musician."

The donkey met an old dog.
"Where are you going?"
asked the donkey.

"My master wants to get rid of me
because I'm too old for hunting,"
said the old dog.

"Come to Bremen with me,"
said the donkey.
"We can be musicians together."

Before long, they met a cat
that was looking very sad.
"What is the matter?"
asked the donkey.

The cat replied, "My master wants
to throw me out because I am old."

"Come with us," said the dog.
"We'll all be musicians together."

11

Further on, they saw a rooster
crying on a farm gate.
"Rooster, why are you crying?"
asked the donkey.

The rooster said, "I am to die.
My master wants to eat me."

The dog shouted, "No!
You cannot let him do that!
Run away with us!"

"Join our band of musicians,"
said the cat.

So the rooster, the cat,
the dog and the donkey
went along the road to Bremen.

14

Night came, and the animals decided
to spend the night in the forest.
The donkey and the dog
sat beneath a tree.
The cat and the rooster
sat in the tree's branches.

Suddenly, the rooster crowed,
"Cock-a-doodle-doo!
I can see a light in a house.
Maybe there is food in there!"

The donkey, the dog, the cat and the rooster
looked through the window
of the brightly lit house.
They saw a gang of thieves
enjoying a delicious dinner.
The animals had an idea.

The donkey placed his front legs
on the windowsill.
The dog got on the donkey's head.
The cat climbed up on the dog.
The rooster sat on the cat's back.
"Time for music!" said the donkey.

HEE-HAW! HEE-HAW! brayed the donkey.

WOOF! WOOF! barked the dog.

MEOW! MEOW! meowed the cat.

COCK-A-DOODLE-DOO! crowed the rooster.

Then with a great crash,
the animals fell through the window
and into the room.

The thieves jumped up,
screaming,

**"It's the Night Ghost
coming to get us!"**

Out those thieves ran,
out into the dark forest.

The animals had a big feast
and then lay down to sleep.
The donkey found some hay in the yard.
The dog lay down behind the door.
The cat sat in front of the stove.
The rooster perched on top of the roof.

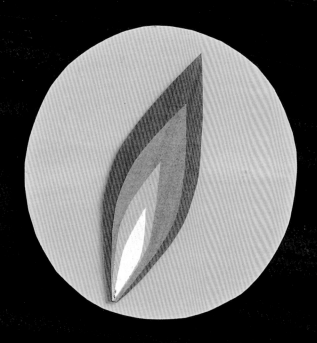

Later that night,
one of the thieves came back
to inspect the house.
It was very dark, so he lit a match.
Something was glowing by the stove.
The thief thought it was a hot coal,
but it was the cat's eye.
When the thief came near
with the match, the cat sprang at him
and scratched his face.

MEOW!

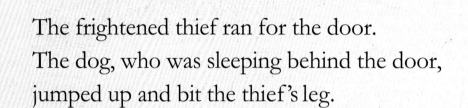

The frightened thief ran for the door.
The dog, who was sleeping behind the door,
jumped up and bit the thief's leg.

WOOF!
WOOF!

Out in the yard,
the donkey kicked the thief.
HEE-HAW! HEE-HAW!

The rooster crowed,

COCK-A-DOODLE-DOO!

The thief cried,
"I'm sorry, Night Ghost!
We will never come back
to this house again."
Then he ran for his life.

The donkey, the dog,
the cat and the rooster
lived happily together
in the house in the forest.